Was It a Good Trade?

for Marie-Celeste

Was It a Good Trade?

By Beatrice Schenk de Regniers

Illustrated by Irene Haas

HarperCollins Publishers

I had a little knife.

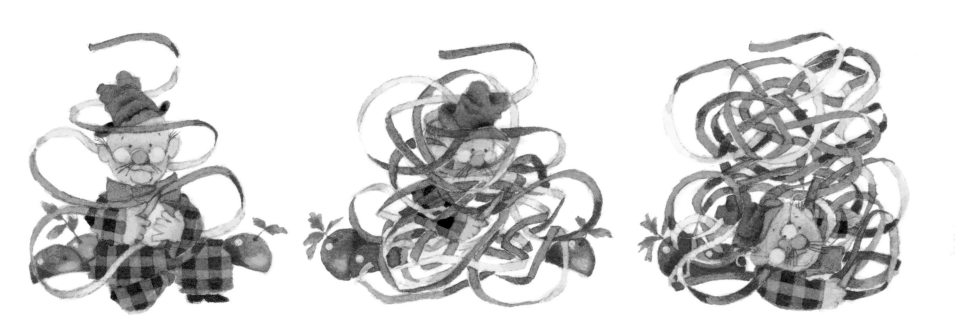

I traded for a wife.

Was it a good trade?
Was it a bad trade?
Was it a good trade~
hey?

My wife baked me a cake.

I traded for a rake.

The rake broke right in two.

I traded for a shoe.

The shoe~it had no mate~

I traded for a slate.

And what I drew on that
I traded for a cat.

Was it a good trade?
Was it a bad trade?
Was it a good trade ~
hey?

The cat she had some kittens.

I traded them for mittens.

The mittens were too big.

I traded for a pig.

The pig's tail would not curl. I traded for a pearl. The pearl was just a phony.

I traded for a pony.

Was it a bad trade?
Was it a good trade?
Was it a bad trade—
hey?

The pony wouldn't budge.

I traded for some fudge.

The fudge was rather stale.

I traded for a whale.

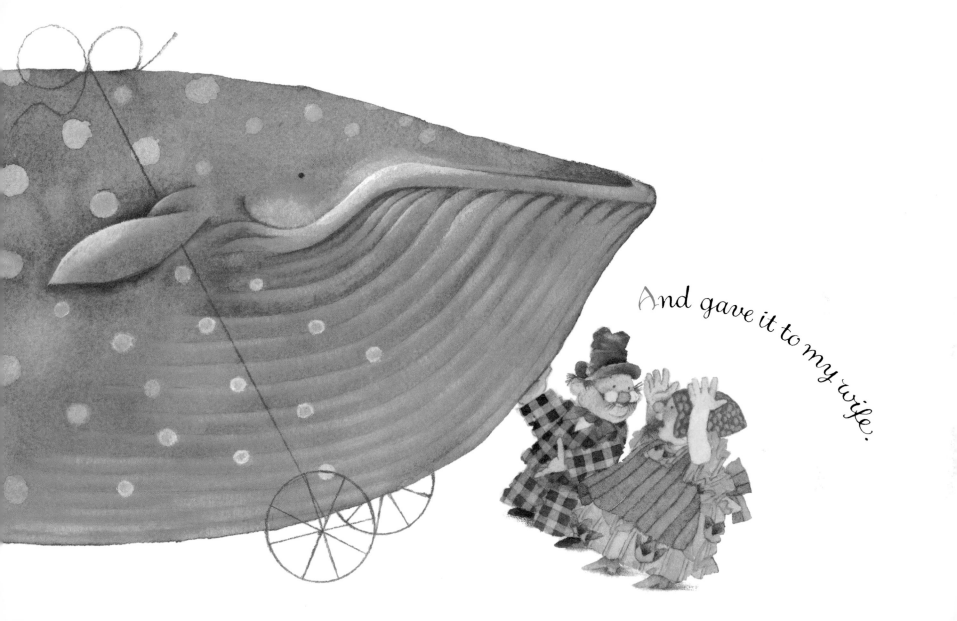

And gave it to my wife.

She traded for a knife.

- So now I have my little knife,

- my little wife,

- and I will keep them all my life.

- I wouldn't trade for a cake a rake

- a shoe a slate

- a cat or kittens

- not even mittens

- not a pig or a pearl

- or a pony or fudge

- or even a whale.

I'm through with trading.

Well...

what've you got to trade?

Was It a Good Trade?

Adapted from a Folk Tune

Seriously

1. I had a lit~tle knife. I trad-ed for a wife.
2. The rake broke right in two. I trad-ed for a shoe.

My wife baked me a cake. I trad-ed for a rake.
The shoe~it had no mate~ I trad-ed for a slate.

Lively

Was it a good trade? Was it a bad trade? Was it a good trade hey?
Was it a bad trade? Was it a good trade? Was it a bad trade hey?

And what I drew on that
I traded for a cat.
The cat she had some kittens.
I traded them for mittens.
    Was it a good trade? etc.

The mittens were too big.
I traded for a pig.
The pig's tail would not curl.
I traded for a pearl.
    Was it a bad trade? etc.

The pearl was just a phony.
I traded for a pony.
The pony wouldn't budge.
I traded for some fudge.
    Was it a good trade? etc.

The fudge was rather stale.
I traded for a whale.
And gave it to my wife.
She traded for a knife.

So now I have my little knife, my little wife,
    and I will keep them all my life.

Library of Congress Cataloging-in-Publication Data
De Regniers, Beatrice Schenk.
Was it a good trade? / by Beatrice Schenk de Regniers ; illustrated by Irene Haas.—1st ed.
p.   cm.
Summary: Never satisfied with what he has, a man trades for a knife, a shoe, and even his
wife, all the while wondering if he has made a good trade.
ISBN 0-06-029359-4 — ISBN 0-06-029360-8 (lib. bdg.)
[1. Contentment—Fiction.   2. Belongings, Personal—Fiction.   3. Stories in rhyme.]
I. Haas, Irene, ill.   II. Title.
PZ8.3.D443 Was   2002
[E]—dc21   2001024320

Hand-lettering by Leah Palmer Preiss
1   2   3   4   5   6   7   8   9   10
❖
First Edition